To Meesh, Tanya, Melinda, Rachelle, Raina, and Gaia, and all the other little girls I hold dear in my heart...

-Pamela Medina Pittman

To Addison and Alexis. Thank you so much for helping Grandma write this book...

-Carol L. Huston

www.mascotbooks.com

When Little Girls Dream

For more information, please contact:
Mascot Books
620 Herndon Parkway #320
Herndon, VA 20170
info@mascotbooks.com

Library of Congress Control Number: 2019900709

CPSIA Code: PRT0519A
ISBN-13: 978-1-64307-071-1

Printed in the United States

When Little Girls Dream

Carol L. Huston & Pamela Medina Pittman

illustrated by Ingrid Lefebvre

When little girls dream...
The **whole** world is pink and glittery.

When little girls dream...

Baby mice
wear hula hoops.

When little
girls dream...

Swings
magically
push
themselves
higher
and
higher.

When little girls dream...

Mermaids
swim in the
bathtub with me.

When little girls dream...
Bananas
wear pajamas.

When little girls dream...
I can **stay up** as late as I want to.

When little girls dream...

Broken hearts can be glued back together.

When little girls dream…
Puppies and kittens
never, **ever** grow up.

When little
girls dream...
Snowflakes fall in
all the colors
of the rainbow.

When little girls dream...
I can visit the man in the moon **every night.**

When little girls dream...
Broccoli tastes
like cotton candy
and melts in your mouth.

When little girls dream...
Whales make waffles and
spout maple syrup.

When little girls dream...
Princesses throw
pajama parties.

When little girls dream...

Best friends last forever.

When little girls dream...
Anything is possible.

About the Authors

Carol L. Huston is a university professor who has taught nursing for 37 years. She lives in northern California and enjoys spending time with her three young grandchildren, who inspired her to write this book.

Pamela Medina Pittman lives in northern California with her husband and two dogs.